I0627438

The Scrapbook of Poems

The Scrapbook of Poems

TSP

The Scrapbook of Poems

TSP

TSP

The Scrapbook of Poems

The Scrapbook of Poems

The Scrapbook of Poems

TSP

The Scrapbook of Poems

TSP

TSP

The Scrapbook of Poems

The Scrapbook
of Poems

Sabina Cardenas

A LATTE & STORIES PUBLISHING

Sabina Cardenas

These are a series of poems I wrote about my favorite person. They were written at different times in the first year of our relationship. I also love scrapbooks, and I wanted to make one for him. He told me it would be a good idea to let the rest of the world have an opportunity to make their own. I hope you like my poetry scrapbook.

Poems:

1. *Falling for You*
2. *September Thoughts*
3. *October Thoughts*
4. *Time Passing By*
5. *Simple*
6. *Old As Time*
7. *Pebbles*
8. *Bad Luck?*
9. *Until We Are No More*
10. *Perfect Love Story*
11. *Different*
12. *The Love of All My Loves*
13. *Flaws*

Instructions:

1. Read the poem and think of a memory with your partner that the poem reminds you of.

2. Add a picture on every camera you see:

3. Write dates or the place on the empty lines on top of the pictures.

4. Make this scrapbook your own.

Falling for You

We are miles and miles apart,
I don't feel it as much as I thought,
One call away, there you are,
Smiling at me waiting to talk,

Waiting to talk about our days,
Make each other feel okay,
Life's never perfect every day,
But when I'm with you, you make me it feel that way,

You're attractive. Yes, you are,
I'll admire you even from afar,
You, hidden gem in the dark,
That I want to keep and never give up,

I think about you and smile,
I think about your nervous face, and I crumble,
I can't believe how much I like you,
Please tell me I will always have you.

You are so nice and sweet

you made my heart

skip a beat

I think about you

A lot

Like a lot a lot

September Thoughts

I met you in September
A regular month
Patriotic for some and
For some it's not

You were so nice and sweet
You made my heart skip a beat
You made me feel comfortable and at peace
You're the one I need

I think about you a lot
Your smile and eyes fill my thoughts
You're so pure at heart
You feel like rare art

This year was different
This month was it
The time to give my heart
That time was now and the time was it.

I LOVE

YOU

MY BEST

FRIEND

October Thoughts

October came, a scary month,
Your favorite one,
The time for mummies and goths,
The time for candies and scares
For me, it was rare,
I met a boy as sweet as a teddy bear

Time starts to get a little colder
I wish you were with me to keep me warmer
I don't know how much time I can be without you
I want December to come faster

I want to see the boy in the costume
The one that smiles at the camera with passion
I know you want to see me too, I assume,
Your eyes are telling me all of the truth

Time will fly, and we will see each other,
A most awaited time for us both
Perfect like the love we have for one another,
In time, the time will not be a bother

Baby

Baby

baby

baby

baby

baby

baby

baby

baby

baby

baby

Baby

baby

baby

Baby

baby

baby

Baby

baby

baby

baby

baby

baby

baby

baby

baby

Time Passing By

As time passes by
I can't deny my love for you

You are funny
You are kind
You are generous
You are one of a kind

I'm grateful to have you
I'm sacred to lose you
I can't imagine a future without you
Without your silly jokes
And without your goofy smile

I'll continue to love you
I'll continue to wait for you
Until then, my love for you will grow and grow
I hope you treasure my heart
The same way I treasure yours.

The
Scrapbook of
Poems

The
Scrapbook of
Poems

Simple

I'm not great with talking,
You're not great with words,
Somehow someway, we make it work,
We talk to each other about everything,
And even more,
I don't think I've ever met someone,
So open, so kind, and pure,
To share everything with me and more,
I'm shock and starstruck,
To meet someone so close to my soul.

YOU

YOU

Old As Time

When your soft skin turns wrinkly,
And your hair turns gray,
I'll be by your side every step of the way

I'll help with your back pain,
And will feed you delicious food,
I know you are capable of doing it yourself, but
I want to do those things for you,

I will love you every morning,
I'll think of you in the afternoons,
I will cuddle you in the evenings,
While we lay on the couch in the living room,

When our skin turns wrinkly
And our hair turns gray
I hope you will love me the same way
As I will love you every day

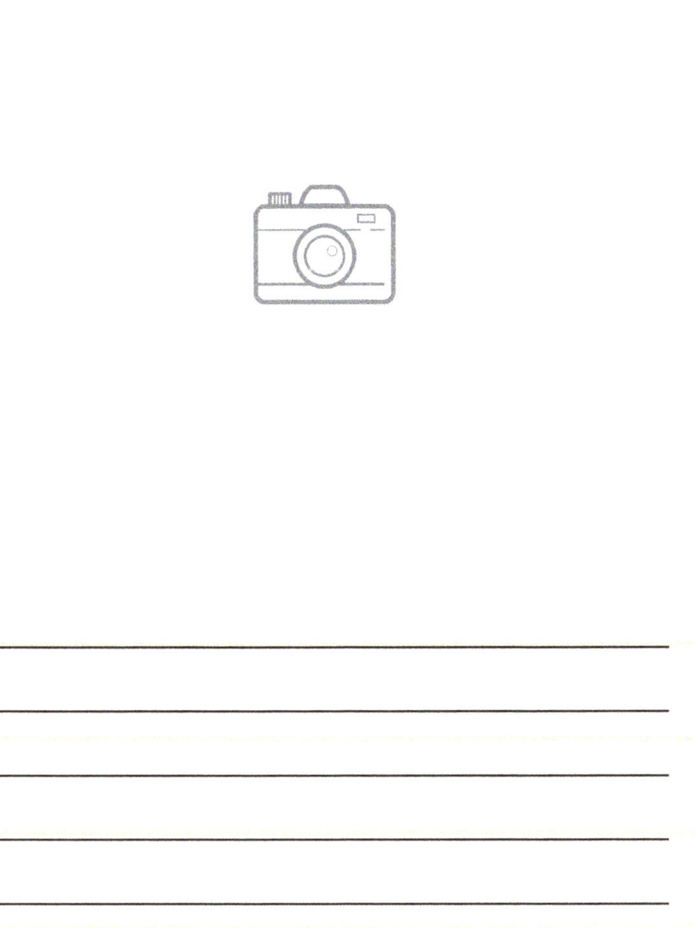

Pebbles

I will love you for every pebble I see on the floor
And for every fork I see in sight
There will always be forks and pebbles as décor
And the love from me will be as shiny and bright

Shiny as a fork
Bright as a pebble
My love for you will always be a rock
And it will become a rebel
A rebel that will fight with all its might
For that once in a lifetime love

They will treasure it and love it
For the rest of their lives
No one will ever deny is a strong love
That people will become jealous of
This kind of love

Bright as a pebble
Shiny as a fork
My heart has an owner
And I love him so

ME
+
YOU
ME
+
YOU

ME
+
YOU

ME
+
YOU

Bad Luck?

You might think we have bad luck
For many dates we've planned have sucked
We don't think like you all
Because time with each other is worth it all

We went to Universal and it was fun
It rained, it was cold, and we were stunned
We were hungry and upset
We couldn't get a win that day

We went to Disney late
We slept on the way on the train
It was almost a night date
But it was one of my favorites yet

We wanted to have a picnic and it was too cold
We wanted to have one in July and it was hot
We couldn't with the weather too white and too gold
But my love for you just grew more

We didn't get to do everything we planned
We were tired and sleepy most of the time
Yet, my love for you kept its stand
I don't want anyone else, but my man

Until We Are No More

I want to be honest with you and tell you
I never knew it was going to start like this

I never knew that the boy I met online
Would be my lover for all times
The good ones and the bad ones
The person that would be by my side

I think about you, and I want to cry
Because I miss so much it hurts
I don't want to be away from you anymore
But I know you have a duty that needs to be served

It's crazy to think that you come from a pool of uncertainty
Yet, the only certain thing in my life is how I feel about you
An instant connection I felt
The moment you messaged me

Some people might call me crazy to trust you as much as I do
But my heart is at peace with or without the distance
My love for you doesn't trouble me
It doesn't cost me doubt
It just causes me sadness when you're not around

I want to be honest and tell the world
That I will love you until we are no more
I want to hold your hand and live every crazy thing possible
Because you're my partner in crime, you're the love of my life

An instant

connection I felt

The moment you

messaged me

It causes me pain when
you're not around

Perfect Love Story

I've never thought of myself as perfect
I am a work in progress, but I am worth it
I know it might take forever to get there
But I want to get there with you by my side

I see your face and I see a dream
A dream so sweet I want to keep
I know your just a human being
But I love you so much, it makes me feel glee

I never want to lose you and for our love to go sideways
I want to keep you close always
So, know that on my side,
I will always try to keep you happy

I know I am not perfect and I will never will be
But I want to try my best for you, honey
So, let's try together at this little thing called life
I promise to keep you in the story as the love of my life

Hey(:

I want to grow with you

Different

We are different people, I know that
Our skins are different colors
We have different cultures
Yet, that doesn't matter to me

I want to love you and respect you for who you are
I never want you to change
I want to grow with you, be there for you
And heal your pain

I know I will never know what's like to be you
You will never know what's like to be me
But we understand each other simply
The differences don't have to keep us at a distance

Even if we're different, we will do this together
I don't want to do this with anyone, but you
Respect, love, and trust is all I want forever
I hope you walk the path I will walk in cue

The love of My loves

You might not be my first love
But you will always be the biggest one
You might not be my first kiss
But I want you to be my last

I will never love anyone the way I love you
My heart beats just for you
Cute and handsome Marque, that's all that I want
I hope you want me as much as I want you

You are the love of my loves, the greatest one
From all the loves and lost
And all the stories that have come across my life
You will always be the biggest one

The purest I love you's
The warmest hugs
The saddest goodbyes
The happiest hi's, that money cannot buy
Came from you, my biggest love
The love of all my loves

The happiest hi's

that money can't buy

The purest I love you's

Flaws

I don't like the way I look in photos,
But I like your face in them
I'm not a big fan of my face,
but I know you like it when
I smile back at you

Your rose color lenses make me feel special
And I feel very sentimental
Every time you look into my eyes

In your eyes, I see honesty,
I see my future
I feel the warmth of your love
And it makes me feel like I need nothing more

So, as I continue to look in the mirror
and find flaws
I know that to you, those flaws
make me look beautiful

You're my biggest fan, and I'm yours
Together forever, that's what I hope

I love pictures of you in them <3

I love being with you <3

ideas for your poem to get you started:

- Think about your favorite things about your partner.
- Your favorite times together.
- The way they make you feel.
- Your relationship goals.
- Your favorite memories.

Write Your Notes Here:

Write your poem notes here:

It's Your Turn(:

Write a poem for your your fav person

____

____

____

____

____

____

____

____

____

____

____

____

I LOVE YOU

I hope you filled this poem scrapbook with your favorite memories with your favorite person, the same way I did with mine. Make it your own and if you can, take pictures and tag me on social media, so that I can see your lovely works!

Sabina xo

I want to love you

&

respect you

I see your face &

I see a dream

book of poems

book of poems

book of poems

book of poems

book of poems

book of poems

book of poems

book of poems

book of poems

book of poems

book of poems

book of poems

book of poems

book of poems

book of poems

book of poems

A Book of Poems

Time with you <3

I promise to keep you

in the story

as the love of my life

I

love

moments

with

you

You might not be
my first love,
but you will
always be the
biggest.

I'M HAPPY WHEN I'M WITH YOU

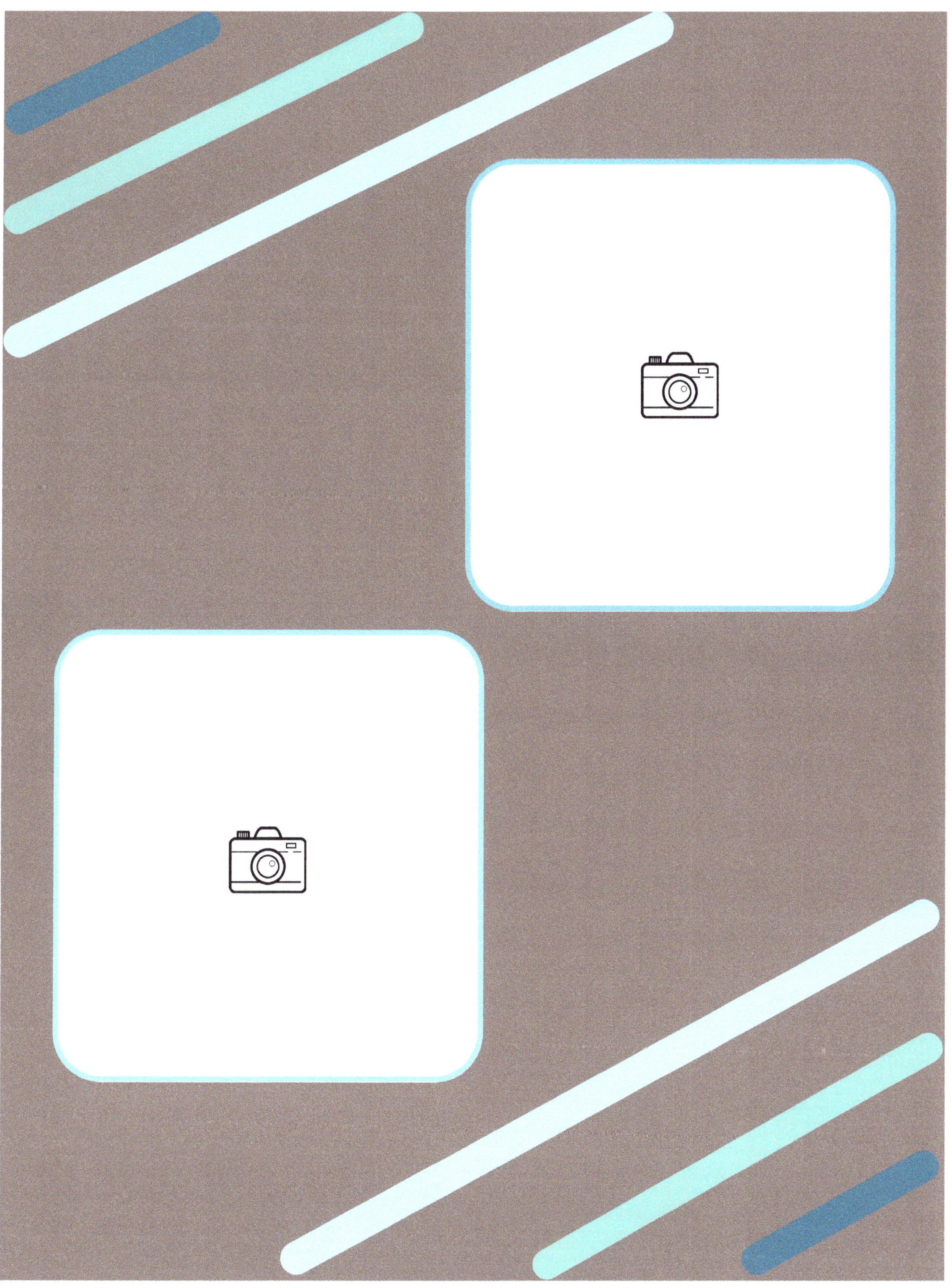

You make me smile

My fav person(:

____

____

The Scrapbook of Poems

The Scrapbook of Poems

TSP

The Scrapbook of Poems

TSP

TSP

The Scrapbook of Poems

The Scrapbook of Poems

The Scrapbook of Poems

TSP

The Scrapbook of Poems

TSP

TSP

The Scrapbook of Poems

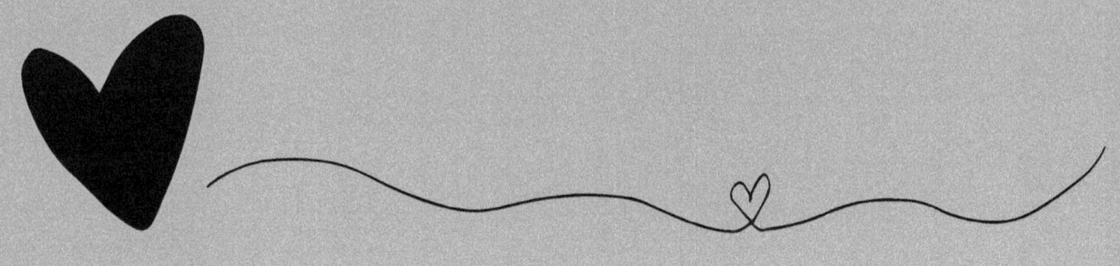

ILY SM

ILY SM

ILY SM

Hey cutie(:

I love you(:

About the Author

Sabina Cardenas is a writer currently living in San Antonio, Texas. She is the author of The Purple Scrapbook: A Book of Poems and her self-published book, A Place to Call Home, which was published on August 21st, 2023. This is her 2nd publication, but has received recognition for her writing in college, being awarded 3rd place for her short story, Infinity, at the Lamar Bruni Vergara Conference in 2018.

Sabina was born in Berwyn, Illinois, and raised in Sabinas Hidalgo, Nuevo Leon, Mexico. She began writing at a young age in Spanish, but as she grew up and moved to Texas, she began writing in English. The predominantly Hispanic/Latino community has influenced her writing. You can see that in her book, A Place to Call Home, as the main characters are Latinos themselves.

Sabina knew from a young age that she wanted to be a writer. She studied English literature at Texas A&M International University, and after graduating, she decided to work on editing her first book. Sabina recently returned to the United States after living in South Korea for over two years. While in Korea, she spent their time working as an ESL teacher and developing new ideas for her next book.

Sabina is currently working on her sequel to A Place to Call Home. She is also working on fantasy and post-apocalyptic stories that readers should keep an eye out for in the near future.

Follow me on Social Media

If Tiktok/Instagram are not your thing... I'm on

Facebook

&

Goodreads

This is another project I wrote and worked on. I would be honored if you would consider reading my novel.

Synopsis:
Millie has lived her entire life in the St. Nicholas of Bali Orphanage, but she knows something is missing. With nothing but a small backpack, her favorite doll, and a letter from her mother containing a photo of her three siblings, Millie embarks on a journey to find her family. On the way, she discovers that her siblings have been separated and living in difficult circumstances, and she must bravely connect the past in order to build a better future. With courage and determination, Millie and her siblings must persevere to create a place to call home.

www.ingramcontent.com/pod-product-compliance
Lightning Source LLC
Chambersburg PA
CBHW041148300726
48978CB00017B/1426